Our Big Little Place

written by
JAMES A. CONAN

illustrated by
Nicolle Lalonde

annick press
toronto • berkeley

Sometimes I hear Mom and Dad talking,
and they say our place is too small.

But it always seems big to me.

It's in a big building, with a lot of people living in it, and other big buildings just like it are all around us. If you look outside the window, past the balcony, there's a whole city.

I like it because it's like everyone in the whole world is right there for me to see.

At night it's still bright, and the lights
only stop where the sky starts.

Sometimes the night feels big and scary, especially right before bed.

Mom and Dad say lots of things seem different when we're sleepy, but the sky's the same size and so am I.

I always feel better once they tuck me in.

My favorite game to play in the morning is hide and seek.

The only way to make it fair is to do it in the dark, with the blinds closed.

Dad puts cushions around the coffee table, so he can look for me without bumping his legs before he goes to work.

Other times, we play basketball.
There's a little net on the door.

The ball is small and soft, so I don't break anything.

Mom can dunk, but my free throw is better.

Playing in the kitchen is the best.

There's lots of wet stuff in the fridge. And dry stuff.

And when you mix the wet stuff and the dry stuff, you get gross, goopy stuff.

Sometimes Mom says I can't play
in the kitchen anymore.

"Why don't we get some fresh air?" she says.

There's a nice park outside, between the big buildings. Mom says it's our backyard.

It's where I go to play with all my friends,
and now they call it that too.

Lauren and Isaac live in the same building
as me, but Michael and Julie don't.

I know where they live though, and when we can't play together, I can wave hello to them in their buildings from the window.

Except when its rainy and foggy out.

Our place only feels small to me when
I can't go out to play, like this morning.

I woke up to say bye when Mom and Dad
left for work, and the weather was bad.

Aunt Elizabeth came over to stay with me.

She wouldn't play basketball with me for long.

I got sooo bored, but then I had an idea.

I called Lauren and Isaac, and we met in the hall.

We had the whole floor to ourselves.

A big, square racetrack.

Start your engines!

Watch out for the corners!

Oh, and the people coming out of the elevators.

After that, Aunt Elizabeth said
I had to come back inside for a bit.

My friends all had to go home, and I couldn't go
back out, so I just went to play with Pixel.

We took the laundry basket with no clothes in it and imagined it was my spaceship. Pixel came with me.

Kitties make the best copilots. Blastoff!

We ended up getting
lost in space.

It was scary, but Dad came and got
us when he got home from work.

It wasn't bedtime yet, so I pretended the living room table was a pirate ship and asked Dad to play with me.

"Whaddaya mean, no?

C'monnnn.

Pretty please?

It'll just be for a minute."

"Ha. Avast!"

Dad's the best at playing pirate.

Sometimes Dad's a pirate with me, and when Mom gets home she's his first mate.

Aunt Elizabeth pretends she's a giant squid,
and we all chase her across the ocean.

That's when I don't mind feeling small.

Here in our big little place.

To my Aunt Elizabeth
—JAC

For Debbie and Rick
—NL

© 2019 James A. Conan (text)

© 2019 Nicolle Lalonde (illustrations)

Designed by Paul Covello

Annick Press Ltd.

We acknowledge the support of the Canada Council for the Arts and the Ontario Arts Council, and the participation of the Government of Canada/la participation du gouvernement du Canada for our publishing activities.

Library and Archives Canada Cataloguing in Publication

Title: Our big little place / written by James A. Conan ; illustrated by Nicolle Lalonde.

Names: Conan, James A., 1990- author. | Lalonde, Nicolle, 1992- illustrator.

Identifiers: Canadiana (print) 20190068922 | Canadiana (ebook) 20190068973 | ISBN 9781773213170 (hardcover) | ISBN 9781773213163 (softcover) | ISBN 9781773213200 (PDF) | ISBN 9781773213187 (EPUB) | ISBN 9781773213194 (Kindle)

Classification: LCC PS8605.O5545 O97 2019 | DDC jC813/.6—dc23

Published in the U.S.A. by Annick Press (U.S.) Ltd.

Distributed in Canada by University of Toronto Press.

Distributed in the U.S.A. by Publishers Group West.

Printed in China

annickpress.com   jamesconan.blog   nicollelalonde.com

Also available as an e-book. Please visit annickpress.com/ebooks for more details.